This book belongs to:

_____

_____

A catalogue record for this book is available
from the British Library

Published by Ladybird Books Ltd
80 Strand London WC2R 0RL

3 5 7 9 10 8 6 4 2

A Penguin company

© Disney MMI

Based on the Pooh stories by

A.A Milne (copyright The Pooh Properties Trust)

LADYBIRD and the device of a Ladybird are trademarks
of Ladybird Books Ltd

Printed in China

Tiggers hate
to lose

Ladybird

Rabbit

Pooh

Piglet

Roo

bridge

water

Eeyore

wood

Tigger

stick

Tigger was bouncing
in the wood.

He saw Pooh and Rabbit
and Eeyore and Piglet
and Roo. They were on
the bridge.

"What are you doing?"
asked Tigger.
"We are playing Pooh
Sticks," said Piglet. "Look!"

"One, two, three... go!"
said Rabbit.

They all threw their sticks
into the water.

Eeyore's stick came under
the bridge first. He won
the game.

"Can I play Pooh Sticks, too?" asked Tigger.
"Yes," said Pooh.

Tigger bounced into the
wood to get some sticks.

 11

Tigger bounced back to
the bridge.
"Tiggers love to play Pooh
Sticks," he said.

"One, two, three... go!"
said Rabbit.

They all threw their sticks
into the water.

"Did I win?" asked Tigger.
"No," said Eeyore.
"I won."

"Let's play again,"
said Tigger.

 15

So they played again.
Eeyore's stick came
under the bridge first.

Tigger was cross.
"Let's play again,"
he said.

So they played again.
And Eeyore won that
game, too.

Eeyore won the next
game, and the next game,
and the game after that.

Tigger was now very cross.

He stamped his foot.
"Let's play again," he said.

So they played again.
And Eeyore won that
game, too.

 21

Tigger was now very, very cross. He threw down his sticks.

"Tiggers don't like Pooh Sticks!" he said.

Tigger stamped off into
the wood. He was so cross
he had no bounce at all.

23

Eeyore went after Tigger.
"You can have my stick,"
said Eeyore. "See if you
can win with that."

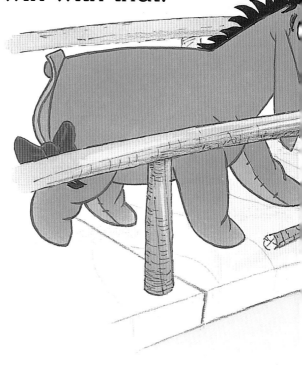

Tigger went back to the bridge. This time he threw Eeyore's stick.

And this time Tigger won.
He was so happy he
began to bounce again.

"Tiggers like Pooh Sticks!"
said Tigger. "But they like
Eeyore best of all!"